To: Noah
A magical story
for a magical you

From:

Oh no!
The wizards
were in
BIG trouble!

A wicked witch had cast
an evil spell completely covering
their magical kingdom in
slimy and extremely smelly goo!
ALL of the wizards were trapped!

4

The wizards really needed
someone to help them catch
the wicked witch,
but who?

5

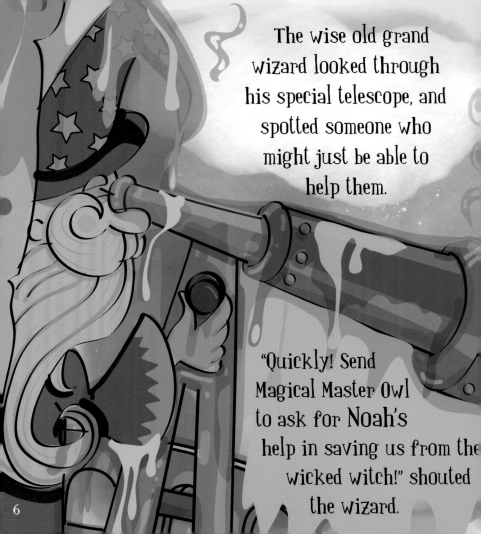

The wise old grand wizard looked through his special telescope, and spotted someone who might just be able to help them.

"Quickly! Send Magical Master Owl to ask for Noah's help in saving us from the wicked witch!" shouted the wizard.

6

Magical Master Owl knew he had
to help so he flapped and fluttered
as swiftly as he could to find the boy
spotted through the telescope.

"WHIZZ BAM !"
Noah said, as he waved
his pretend wand towards
his dog Ruffles.

"Oh Ruffles you are
supposed to turn into a
flying dog."

Noah SO wanted
to be a Wizard.

8

Suddenly with a flitter and a flap, Magical Master Owl squawked through **Noah's** window into the bedroom and explained (in his best owlish) the trouble the wizards were in, and asked a shocked **Noah** if he could help.

"Of course!" said a delighted Noah.

So Magical Master Owl squawked three times, flapped his wings four times, and with a WHIZZ PUFF, a broomstick, cape and magic wand suddenly appeared!

10

Noah put on the cape,
picked up the wand,
and jumped on his brand
new broomstick.

Quick as a flash
they zoomed out of
Noah's window to look
for the wicked witch.

11

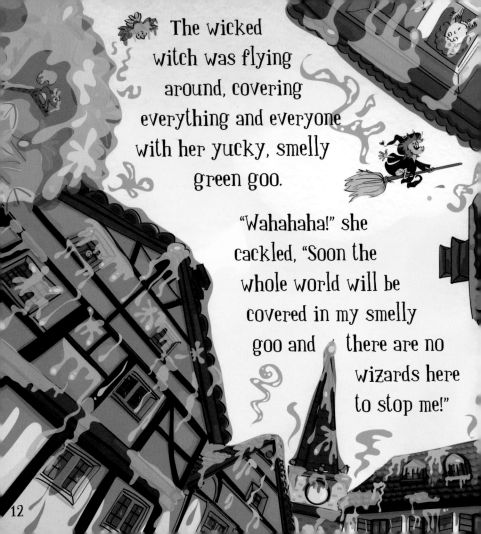

The wicked witch was flying around, covering everything and everyone with her yucky, smelly green goo.

"Wahahaha!" she cackled, "Soon the whole world will be covered in my smelly goo and there are no wizards here to stop me!"

ut little did she
realize that Noah
was on his way.

He zoomed
under bridges...

...and over houses,
looking for the
goo-spreading
witch.

Suddenly Ruffles made
a big booming **bark**.
His super-smelling nose had caught
a whiff of the wicked witch, but she
was too far away for **Noah**
to cast a spell on her.

Noah clicked his heels, gripped his broomstick even tighter, and zoomed at supersonic speed towards the wicked witch.

Finally Noah caught up with the wicked witch.

"Who are you?" the wicked witch sneered, as she launched a massive dollop of sticky green goo at Noah.

With lightning speed
Noah waved his magic wand.
"BIZZ POP GOO I will stop you!" he shouted.
A huge brightly-colored umbrella appeared,
deflecting all of the smelly goo.

17

The wicked witch squealed with anger, zapping another dollop of smelly green goo towards **Noah**.

"WHIZZ SPLAT send me your hat!" **Noah** shouted.

The witch's hat flew off her head, catching all of her smelly green goo. Yuck!

The witch couldn't believe what this boy wizard was doing!

18

"ZIP ZAP, you will be trapped in your hat!" Noah cast another spell.

The witch's goo-filled hat flew back to her, squashing down over her head, squishing her in the smelly green goo.

Hurray the wicked witch was trapped!

A triumphant **Noah** took the wicked witch back to the wizards' castle.

All the slippery, slimy green goo had now gone thanks to **Noah** breaking the bad witch's horrible spell.

The wizards were so grateful to
Noah that they let him keep the cape,
broomstick AND magic wand!

Noah finally felt like a true wizard!

The End